Curly Girl Adventures

Tangled

L. B. Anne

JOA PRESS
FLORIDA

TANGLED

ISBN: 9798689314952

Contents

No More Parties

My name is Zuri. I don't like names that start with a Z, but I like mine because it means good, nice, pretty, lovely, and cute. All of that is definitely me. I'm seven years old, and—

"Zuri, tell the truth."

"But that's how I always start the story."

"Then you weren't telling the truth. Start again," said my mom.

I blew air hard out of my nose.

My name is Zuri. I don't like names that start with a Z, but I like mine because it means good, nice, pretty, lovely, and cute. All of that is definitely me. I am not seven years old. I'm six, but only because my birthday is always late. That's why. Everybody in my class turns seven before me.

It's no fun having your birthday two days after Christmas. I want a birthday gift and a Christmas gift—not both combined and not on the same day.

"AH HA! Zuri hasn't had a party," that beetle-faced Josh said last year.

When my birthday finally came, guess what? We were on winter break.

Shh... Open your eardrums. I've got a secret, that's why. I'm moving my birthday up this year. I can if I want. It's my right for living in the United States of America. I'm going to have two parties. One at school and one at the Princess Beauty salon, near Sea World. And if it doesn't happen, I'm going to protest like Martin Luther King Jr. I already knew about him, but my class learned about his protests during Black History Month.

Today, I sat with my arms folded while that new
Z kid's mom handed out cupcakes for his birthday.

There are too many Z names in my class now. There's me, Zoey, and Zach.

Zach's birthday is late in the year also, but not as late as mine.

Beetle-faced Josh dipped his finger in his cupcake and licked the blue frosting off. Then, he stuck his tongue out at me, so I could see it.

I ignored that guy and put my elbows on the desk, holding my face in my hands. Then, I leaned back in my chair and frowned and grumbled, but no one noticed.

Mr. Bugsby walked over to my desk and squatted next to me as Zach's mom led the class in singing happy birthday. That guy was right near my face, blowing pretzel breath at me.

"Zuri, we're all singing happy birthday to Zach. We've discussed you being nicer to your classmates, remember? Please sing with us."

"She's being mean," said Josh. His bushy blond hair grew back fast after his haircut for picture day—mostly the bangs. He pushed them out of his eyes putting blue frosting in his hair.

4

Mr. Bugsby stood, and I frowned up at him as he sang, "Happy birthday to Za-ach, happy birthday to Zach. How old are—"

"I will not! I will not sing another happy birthday until *I* have a birthday at school!"

Mr. Bugsby knelt beside my seat again. "Zuri, you are too old for these tantrums. A seven-year-old should not—"

"I'm not seven. I'm six."

That guy looked like he didn't believe me.

"I haven't had a birthday yet."

"I didn't realize that. Well, six-year-old Zuri—"

"Shh… Don't say that so loud."

"I would like you to participate," Mr. Bugsby continued. "Or should I remind you I have your parents on speed dial?"

My eyes grew big like a tarsier. The class watched a film about them. They're kind of like monkeys. They're small, have huge eyes, and they eat grasshoppers. YUCK!

"How old are you now-ow, how old are you now," I sang as loud as I could. I didn't want to get in trouble before Pickle and I went to Neli's house. We were going to see her new bedroom after school.

Pickle is my best friend and my cousin. She has curly hair like mine, and we yell, "PROUD TO BE CURLY!" when we see each other. That's because we have a club called the Curly Girl Club. We celebrate all types of curly hair, especially our own.

I have more hair than most kids—enough for three kids. Pickle too. Her real name is Pia. But our family has called her Pickle since she was two years old on account of her loving to eat sour pickles. She'll make a throw up face if you offer her the sweet kind.

We live on Cadbury Lane. But Pickle lives way at the other end, and I ride my kick scooter to visit her. Neli lives on my street too, but closer to Pickle's house.

Pickle has, uh—peanut brittle—brittle bone disease. That's what it is. I always have to say peanut brittle, first, to remind myself. The science name for it is Osteogenesis Imperfecta. I finally learned how to pronounce it. It means her bones break easily, and that's real painful. That's why she has to be very careful.

Pickle is the best person in the world. The smartest too.

"Hey, Pickle!" I waved and yelled as I stepped down off the school bus. Pickle whirred through the air and over the trees.

"Watch where you're going!" Ms. Abbie exclaimed.

I stopped and looked around for cars.

Ms. Abbie was my school bus driver. Everyone listened to Ms. Abbie. She wasn't a lot taller than us, but if you were bad, she'd give you a scolding, quick in a hurry. And she had power like the president, because when she stopped the bus, all the cars had to stop and wait until she started driving again.

Pickle landed on my lawn and I took her into my house. Pickle is a drone. Well, she's not *the* drone. She operates it and flies around watching me.

As soon as I walked into my house, I hung up my bookbag and called Pickle on my cell phone.

"Hurry up! We're going to be late," said Pickle, without saying hello.

"I'm on the way."

Neli's Room

When I got home, I ran upstairs looking for my dad. Then, I ran through the living room and kitchen. I found him in his mancave watching golf. He always watched golf shows. Boring!

I leaned over the arm of the sofa and kissed him on the cheek. "Daddy, can I go to Pickle's?"

"You know the rules, be back before the streetlights come on."

"I will," I said, and ran from the room. My dad's off days were the best days, because he only wanted to relax. He didn't mind if I went outside right after school and never remembered to ask about homework.

I carried the drone outside and hopped on my scooter as Pickle flew off. "Wait for me, Pickle!"

My scooter rolled past Kai who sat on her porch biting into an apple. Her little sister sat next to her wearing a fairy costume with wings. "Hi, Zuri!" she said and waved.

I waved back, kicked my leg fast, and sped past Hector.

"Hey, Zuri the Great!"

"Hey, Hector." I had a huge grin for that guy. He remembered my superhero name. That's why.

"PROUD TO BE CURLY!" Pickled yelled with her fist in the air when she saw me. She was sitting outside in her electric wheelchair. Pickle can't walk well, but she's working on it.

"PROUD TO BE CURLY, Curly Girl!" I replied and dropped my scooter. Pickle used her controls to bring her drone down.

"Looking good, *Stacey!*" I said to her curly ponytail. Us Curly Girls had names for our hair. Mine was called *Shelby.*

I held my hands out in front of me.

"What's that?" asked Pickle.

"I'm giving you a ten for your landing."

"Thanks. I'm becoming a pro. Gran, we're ready!"

"Okay, here I come," Gran called from the porch.

I met her at the bottom of Pickle's wheelchair ramp and hugged her. "Hi Gran."

"Hello, Zuri. Are you riding your scooter over?"

"No, I'm going to ride with Pickle."

"Hop on," said Pickle.

I stood on the back of her wheelchair, and she turned toward the corner, so we could cross the street.

"CHARGE!" I screamed as I pointed.

"Don't you dare!" yelled Gran.

Pickle and I couldn't stop laughing at that one.

Neli's house was across the street and a few houses down from Pickle's. "PROUD TO BE CURLY!" she said when she opened the front door.

"PROUD TO BE CURLY," both Pickle and I replied.

"*Susan* looks cute," Pickle said of Neli's hair. Pickle was homeschooled, so it was her first time seeing it.

I had already commented on how beautiful it was at school. Her mom had cornrowed her hair into loose curly puffs.

Neli turned looking behind her. "Mom, they're here!"

"Come in. Come in." Her mom was happy to see us—even me, after the whole hair thing—the time I soaked Neli's straightened hair with a water hose to turn it back curly. Then my pickled pudding creation splashed over her from the blender. I was in big trouble that day.

"How are you girls?" she asked. "You look pretty, Pia."

"Thank you," Pickle replied.

"Something smells good," said Gran.

"Oh, that's just chicken I'm baking for dinner. Neli can't wait for you guys to see her room. Go on up."

Gran carried Pickle, because she can't climb stairs. That's why they don't have an upstairs at their house. I always want to carry her, but the grownups think I'll trip and fall.

Once, when no one was around, Pickle asked me to help her and I carried her for a minute. I didn't fall though.

Gran was careful on the stairs. But I walked with my arms outstretched in case she tripped, and I needed to catch them both.

Neli's bedroom was at the end of the hall.

"WOW!" Pickle and I exclaimed as we walked in. "IT'S BEAUTIFUL!"

Neli's mom had decorated her room with unicorns with blue, purple, and turquoise rainbows, and blue skies, and she used glitter in the paint. Even the ceiling sparkled.

I tried not to be jealous of my friend, but I wished I could switch bedrooms with her.

Neli showed us her fluffy pillows and her craft table and supplies. Then she knocked over a container of glitter by mistake. The lid wasn't on tight. It spilled on the carpet.

Pickle and I crowded in next to her.

To us Curly Girls, it was a beautiful pile of stardust. Neli's mom didn't agree. She brought a hand vacuum to suck it up quick and fast. After she finished, I could still see specks of it in the grey carpet.

"Glitter lives forever," I told Neli.

"No, it doesn't."

"Uh-huh," Pickle agreed.

"Yes, it does," I added. Even after the aparsnips."

Neli's mom looked at Gran and laughed. "Aparsnips?"

"Yes. The end of everything," I replied.

"Ahh… Zuri, do you know what a parsnip is?" Neli's mom asked.

I didn't understand that woman. "No."

"It's a vegetable. It looks like a carrot but it's cream colored."

Pickle and I wrinkled our noses. "Gross."

"Actually, it's pretty tasty. But I think you meant to say apocalypse."

"Yes, that. At the apoca-apocalytical—"

"Apocalypse," corrected Gran.

"At the apocalypse, we will still find glitter everywhere. My mom swept some up, and it was still there months later."

"Neli, don't touch your hair!" her mom yelled.

Too late. I guess Neli had forgotten she hadn't brushed all the glitter from her fingers. Now *Susan* was nice and sparkly.

I thought it was pretty, so I copied her, and Pickle copied me.

Neli's mom turned and looked at us sitting on the floor rubbing our hair. She shook her head. "Do you always have to do what the other does?"

"We're the Curly Girl Club. We always stick together," said Pickle.

"You guys are a curly mess."

We were missing two of our Curly Girls: Kayla and Zoey. We were all in the same grade, but Kayla and Zoey didn't live near us.

"What's the apocalypse?" Neli asked as she flicked glitter from her fingers.

"I've seen it in movies," I explained. "It's in a gazillion years when everything explodes, and spaceships take us to live on Saturn."

"Oh."

"That's enough apocalypse talk," said Neli's mom. "Let's all go and see if we can wash this glitter from our hands."

Glitter Everywhere

Washing our hands didn't get rid of all the glitter.
We still found tiny silver sparkles on our clothes and
faces. Even Gran had a little on her dress.

When I went home, my mom stopped me before
I could run upstairs. "Halt, right there, young lady."

"Halt?"

"Yes. Stay right there."

"Why do I have to—"

"Hello, Mommy," she said, reminding me that I
hadn't greeted her.

"Oops, sorry. Hello, Mommy. Why do I have to
halt?"

My mom looked me over. "What happened to your hair?"

"There's glitter in it."

"I can see that. How did it get in your hair?"

"Isn't it pretty?"

"Zuri…"

"So Neli had glitter out. And her mom was right there. And there was glitter on the floor, and I tripped, and my hair landed in it."

"What have I told you about fibbing?"

"Oh, yeah. I put my hand in the glitter and put it on my hair."

My mom sighed at me.

"Sorry, Mommy."

"Why didn't you tell me the truth when I asked?"

"Because words pop in my head, and I say them as soon as they land there."

The corner of my mom's mouth turned up, and I think she was about to laugh at me. "Let me guess, Pickle is a walking unicorn also?"

I nodded.

"I better get over there and take care of her first. That's too much work for your Gran."

"Lela," my mom called.

"Yes?" she responded from upstairs.

"Run your sister's bath and help her with her hair."

"She doesn't know how," I complained.

"Yes, she does."

Lela ran to the stairs. "Mommy, she never lets me."

"She will today. Won't you?"

"Yes, ma'am," I groaned.

"Get up here, rugrat."

"Mommy, did you hear what that woman called me?"

"Lela, stop name calling. Zuri, let her help. I'm not playing with you guys. I want this done by the time I get back. Go on upstairs for your bath."

I trudged up the stairs and into the bathroom where Lela turned on the tub faucet. She didn't even add any bubbles.

"Don't make it too hot," I insisted.

"Oh, my goodness. Look at your hair!" said Lela. "Don't move. I have to get towels." She stepped out into the hall and took towels from the closet.

"I can see exactly where you've been," she said.

"Why?"

"Because there are specks of sparkles here and they're on the floor all the way into the bathroom." She shook her head. "You and glitter."

Lela acted like my mom sometimes. She made my nerves shake just like beetle-faced Josh did at school. Just because she was in seventh grade, she thought she could tell me what to do all the time.

Lela washed my hair and made me put on my pajamas even though it was too early for bed.

"OUCH!" I screamed every time she tried to detangle my hair. "You don't know what you're doing. Did you spray it with Mommy's leave-in conditioner?"

"I'm doing the same thing I do with mine. I'm finger combing it and detangling it. You're just tender-headed." That meant my scalp was very sensitive and it hurt whenever someone wasn't gentle when styling my hair. It was also the reason I didn't like braids. Just let my hair hang loose. That was good enough for me. And I had so much hair, it took forever to detangle.

Lela knocked my head over to the side.

I swung my hand at her. "Oww, stop it. You can let Mommy finish it," I told her.

"That's fine with me, because I've had enough with you squirming around and pulling away from me. I was only trying to help you anyway. Do you know what would happen if your hair stayed like that?"

Lela neared my face with her eyes squinting and her hands clawed. "It would be like those weeds outside under our shrubs, how you can't see through them down to the dirt. How it chokes out and kills the plants and bugs. Geckos can't even get through them. That's your hair."

"No it's not. Don't say that."

Lela walked away with a sly grin as I sat rubbing my fingers through my hair feeling the curls and then my scalp. When my mom got home, she

21

finished detangling my hair, and it hurt a lot less. But I couldn't stop thinking about what Lela said.

I had such a bad dream that night, and it was all Lela's fault.

I dreamed my hair was all tangled and long and nothing could get through it. It grew over my face, and my mom had a giant comb, but she couldn't get through my hair to help me. And I couldn't walk because of it. I tried to reach out to her, but I couldn't move.

When I woke up, I laid in bed thinking about my dream and looking at the ceiling.

"Zuri, breakfast," my mom called.

I tried to sit up but couldn't move. I pulled and pulled.

"Mommy!" I screamed and cried. The dream was happening in real life. It was all real. "Mommy!"

She came running. "What's wrong?"

Lela stood in the doorway in her pj's with her hand covering her mouth. I think that woman was giggling.

"Help! I can't move! I'm tangled up."

My mom leaned over me and looked back at the door, shaking her head. "Lela!"

"It was just a joke." She laughed like someone was tickling her.

My mom placed my hand on my head and ran it up to the headboard, so I could feel what Lela had done. She had tied my hair to my bedpost while I was sleeping.

I breathed hard out of my nose, having frustration with Lela. I was glad it was just a trick, but I was going to get her back for playing a joke on me. I planned to think up something good while I was at school. The Curly Girls would help me.

Tangled with Josh

That morning at school, Mr. Bugsby left the classroom to help that nosey girl, Jaime, in the hallway. She arrived later than the rest of us and still had to have breakfast. She sat out there, eating a Pop-tart before Mr. Bugsby took attendance.

"Zuri!" Omari yelled, as Mr. Bugsby walked back into the room. Omari is my other best friend—after my Curly Girls. He'd be equal to my Curly Girls if he wasn't a boy.

I zipped around the room, running from beetle-faced Josh. Mr. Bugsby grabbed me quick in a hurry and then Josh as he laughed and reached for me.

Zoey had been chasing Josh. She's a Curly Girl too. She was the one doing all the screaming.

"Stop that running. You guys know the rules. What is going on here?" Mr. Bugsby demanded.

I just knew we were all going to get sent to the office that time.

"I punched Josh because he pulled *Shelby*, and my mom told me never to let anyone—"

"Wait a minute. Did you just say punched?"

"Oops. I did, didn't I? But I didn't punch him hard. And he pulled *Shelby*!"

"No, I didn't!" Josh exclaimed.

"Yes, you did!"

"Yes, you did," Zoey repeated after me.

"Who is Shelby?" asked Mr. Bugsby while looking around the classroom.

Everyone else was seated at their desks looking like they were perfect angels now that Mr. Bugsby was back.

"We don't have a student named Shelby. She must be in the wrong class."

"Shelby is her hair," said Josh.

26

Mr. Bugsby looked surprised and lifted his eyebrows as he looked at my ponytail. "You pulled Zuri's hair?"

"Not on purpose. It's big and always in the way."

Zoey shook her head. "Na-unh, you ran up and pulled her. I saw you."

"And why were you out of your seat, Zoey."

"Because Curly Girls do everything together. It's the rule. PROUD TO BE CURLY!" she exclaimed with her fist in the air.

I shook my head at her, and I think Mr. Bugsby had enough with us. He had frustration on his face and his head fell back and he looked up at the ceiling.

"Zoey, go back to your desk. Zuri and Josh, you come with me."

I looked back at Omari. His eyes were wide. I think that kid was worried for me. I didn't want to cry in front of Josh, but I felt like I might, because I didn't want to go to the principal's office.

Mr. Bugsby took something from the bin next to his desk. Then he took us out in the hall and looked in the window next to the door to make sure everyone was still seated.

"It's all your fault," Josh whispered.

"Oh, be quiet," I told that kid.

"They're whispering," said that nosy Jamie from the table behind us, as she pushed her glasses up on her tiny nose. She did that all day long because her nose was so small.

"Jaime, are you finished with your breakfast?" asked Mr. Bugsby.

She crumpled the silver wrapper and tossed it in the trash can next to the door. "Yes."

"Then you can go inside now."

I've never seen her walk so slow. She watched us as she picked up her backpack and walked into the classroom.

"I'm not taking you to the principal's office today…"

I looked up at Mr. Bugsby, surprised. I almost hugged that guy.

"I thought of something better. You two stand next to each other shoulder to shoulder."

Josh pressed his shoulder into mine. We were about the same height.

What Mr. Bugsby did next, I couldn't believe. He tied my arm and then my leg to Josh's like we were one person. He tangled me up with him.

"Have you lost your mind?" I yelled.

"Zuri!"

"Sorry, Mr. Bugsby. I'm just in shock. Call 911."

"You don't need 911. This is what's going to happen. The two of you will do everything together until you learn how to work together and get along."

"But—"

"Now you can go back to your desks."

"Like this?" asked Josh.

I agreed with that kid this time. "In front of everyone? I think I would rather go to the principal's office."

Mr. Bugsby pointed, and we walked back inside the classroom—skipping forward with our attached legs.

Those kids laughed at us.

"Settle down," Mr. Bugsby instructed. "Have a seat, you two."

Our desks were pushed together, and we argued about how to sit down.

"Follow me," I said."

"No, follow me," Josh said, pulling me backward.

"You're going the wrong way!"

OOF!

We fell back on our bottoms, and the class laughed again.

"One. Two…" Mr. Bugsby began to count. When he did that, boy oh boy, you'd better find your seat and be quiet.

Josh and I stood, and he didn't argue with me this time. I slid across his seat, into mine.

It worked. We were both sitting.

"You could have pulled your chairs back, walked in front of them, and sat down. Then you would only have to scoot together to move them forward," said Omari.

"Now you tell me."

Where is Pickle

The kids in the cafeteria watched us at lunch and giggled.

"PEOPLE! We do not stare! Staring is not polite!" I told them.

I never ate with Josh before. Now I had to watch him chew with his mouth open and listen to him make smacking sounds. I tried to ignore that guy.

During recess we ran together and hung from the monkey bars, with Zoey and Kayla trying to hold Josh's feet up when he felt he couldn't hold on any longer.

Mr. Bugsby untied us at the end of the day, so we could go home. I was glad to be free, like I'd been in jail.

On the school bus, kids snickered as I walked down the aisle looking for a seat.

Noah laughed. "I heard you were Siamese twins with crazy Josh today."

"Omari, how does he know about it? Did you tell?" I asked as I sat behind him.

He shrugged.

"Josh is not crazy. He's hyper," I said over my seat.

"So that wasn't a rumor? It really happened?"

I didn't respond to that guy. I slumped in my seat and looked out of the window all the way home, instead of goofing around with my friends.

But Noah wouldn't shut his big mouth. He kept singing the "Siamese Cat Song" from the *Lady and the Tramp* movie.

I couldn't wait to get off the bus when it stopped. When I hopped down the three steps and stood on the sidewalk, I looked up at the sky and over the trees. I didn't hear any buzzing. Pickle wasn't there. She always flew around waiting for me to get home from school.

"Where's your friend," asked Noah, laughing as he ran past. "Nobody talks to drones anyway."

I stopped walking and thought for a moment. "Oh no. Something may be wrong with Pickle. She may have had a fracture!" I ran as fast as my feet could go and my feet go really fast. No one in my class can beat me in a race.

Our garage was always open when I got out of school. I ran in huffing and puffing.

"MOMMY!" I screamed. "Is Pickle in the hospital? Is she okay? Did she break a bone or a bunch of bones?" I asked all of that really fast.

"Hold on. Slow down. What makes you think that?"

"She wasn't waiting for me today around the bus stop."

"Zuri, is that all? Maybe she had something to do today, or she's not home."

I ran upstairs to my room and checked the big calendar on the back of my bedroom door. I had a schedule just like the one on the back of Pickle's door. Nope. No doctor appointments.

"Something's wrong!" I shrieked. "Pickle didn't answer her phone and Gran didn't answer hers either. They only do that when they're at the hospital."

"Zuri, nothing is wrong. She isn't home. Do you have to know where Pickle is at all times?"

"Yes."

"No, you don't."

My mom patted the back of a chair at the kitchen table. "Sit down here and do your homework."

I ate the string cheese she gave me for my snack. After that, I pulled my notebook from my backpack and read over my spelling words:

Enough

Sometimes

Float

Since

Eight

Wrong

Weather

Rainbow

Then I used each word in a sentence, quick in a hurry, so I could go to Pickle's house.

Enough is enough.

Sometimes it rains.

Float on the ocean.

Since when?

Eight is a number.

Wrong turn.

Weather stories are on the news.

Rainbows are pretty.

Math was next. I took out my math workbook and placed it on the table.

I was minding my own business when Lela walked in and stood behind my chair.

She pointed at my paper. "That's not right and that's not right and that's not right."

"Ugh... Leave me alone."

"Fine. Turn in the wrong answers so everyone thinks you're dumb."

"I'm not dumb."

"I didn't say you were."

"And Mommy said not to use that word."

"You call me stupid all the time. It means the same thing."

"I don't have time for you right now. I have things to do."

"You better have time to correct your answers. You know Mommy or Daddy is going to check them."

She was right. I had been writing down anything just to get it done. I erased all my answers and started again.

After I finished, I called her. "Lela, look. Can you check them?"

"You want *me* to check them?"

"Please."

"You said please *to me*?

"Is this a trick?" she asked as she looked around like I had a bucket of paint floating in the air waiting to pour over her head or something. I held the workbook out to her.

Lela took the book from me and leaned over the counter checking my answers. "They're right," she said and placed the book back on the table.

I hopped up from my seat. "Good. Thank you."

"You said thank you *to me*? Why didn't I have my phone out to record all of this. Mommy is not going to believe it."

No Friends

I ran out to the garage and jumped on my scooter, ignoring the kids outside playing as I sailed by. Lauren and Ashley jumped rope. The two boys who were usually wrestling in their yard, begged them for a rope, so they could pull something with it.

DING! DING! DING! DING! DING! DING!

I kept pressing on the doorbell until someone answered Gran's door.

"Gran! You're here! Why haven't you answered your phone?"

"I'm sorry, sweetie. Did you call? It's on the charger."

Gran had such an old phone and didn't want a new one. I was surprised it worked at all. She walked away from the door. "Are you coming inside?"

"Where is Pickle?"

"Oh, she's over at Neli's."

"At Neli's? Why is she over at Neli's?"

"They've been spending more time together."

"What? Why?"

Gran responded, but I didn't hear what she said because I ran across the street to Neli's house. She and Pickle were in the backyard.

"Hey, Zuri. PROUD TO BE CURLY!" Neli exclaimed with her fist up.

"Yeah, yeah, yeah." I gave Neli my mean face and shook my body at her.

Neli frowned. "What's wrong?"

"Pickle, come home. Now!"

"Why? Does my dad want me home?"

I blocked off Neli so she couldn't hear what I whispered. "You should be playing with me at your house right now."

"You can play with us here."

"Yeah," said Neli with a grin.

I let out the growl that I get in trouble for at school.

"Oh boy, she's angry," said Pickle.

I stormed out of the backyard and hopped on my scooter.

It wasn't fair. We had the most kids on any street. Neli could've chosen anyone else to play with, but she chose my Pickle. I had wanted us to look for turtles near the creek that afternoon.

I rode down to the end of my street and stopped when I saw Noah and Kai. They held Super Soaker water blasters and sprayed any kid they saw.

I slowed down as I got close. "Don't do it," I whispered.

Those kids just looked at me. They never did that. Now *they* didn't want to play with me?

"What are you waiting for? Come on. Chase me," I yelled.

"Why?" asked Noah.

"Because you have your Super Soakers."

"No way, Jose. Your mom will snap."

That was true. She'd snapped before when I got soaked from a water balloon fight. But that was only because we were going out to dinner and I let myself get wet in the five minutes it took for my parents to come out to the car.

Hector ran from behind a house. "There he is," Noah yelled. "Get him."

Kai took off after him.

I rode home with my head hanging low, let my scooter fall to the ground, and kicked it. My mom heard the garage door close when I came in the house.

"Did you find Pickle?"

I ran into her arms in tears. "Yes."

"Zuri, what happened?"

"Pickle is not my friend anymore."

"Since when?"

"Since today. She has all new friends and no time for me."

My mom rubbed my hair. "I'm certain that's not the case. You guys are so close."

"Not anymore."

"You're right," said my mom.

"I know I am."

"How dare she!"

"That's what I'm saying." I was glad she was on my side.

"Pickle is homeschooled, and it's always just her, Gran, and your Uncle Frank. But you are out and about with all your friends, up and down the street, and seeing them in school. Plus, you have a whole classroom full of friends. Is it fair for you to have many and for Pickle to only have one?"

My mom walked away, and I stood there with my mouth open. I hadn't thought about all that stuff. Now I felt bad for the way I acted.

It was the worst day ever. I didn't go back outside. Instead, to make myself feel better, I made a list of things for my secret birthday party. It had to take place before Thanksgiving break. "I'm a bubblehead," I said while slapping my forehead. "I forgot about the cake. How am I going to take a cake to school?"

"What are you doing?" asked Lela.

"Minding my business."

"You're being such a snot."

"That's why I have a secret and I'm not telling you. Na-na-nana," I sang as I waved my paper at her.

She snatched it from me, and I chased her.

"Mommy, tell Zuri to leave me alone."

Lela held the paper over her head as I jumped, trying to reach it.

"Give it back! Okay then. You asked for it."

"EIYEE!" Lela screamed as I landed on her.

I'd climbed up on the couch and jumped onto her back reaching for the paper.

"Look, Woman, give me back my paper before I—"

"Zuri! Lela!"

We froze in place hearing my mom's voice and then her footsteps from upstairs.

"She's coming," I whispered.

OOF!

Lela flipped over the sofa with me still on her back. "Shh... Just lay there and be quiet," she told me.

My mom walked around the sofa, and we crawled around the side.

"You do know I can see you, right? I'll take those cell phones."

"Noooo..." Lela and I said, as we reached in our pockets.

My mom took our phones and put them in her purse. "I've had enough of you guys arguing. Come here."

We followed her into the kitchen.

GASP!

She began to tie us together like Mr. Bugsby had tied me and beetle-faced Josh at school. And my dad just stood there watching and nodding in agreement.

"That's right," my mom said. "Mr. Bugsby called and told me about you and Josh. I thought it was a great idea."

"Now you and Lela can learn to work together too," Daddy added.

"Mommy, I can't do this," Lela complained. "I have soccer practice."

"Yeah, she does," I added, trying to help.

"I guess Zuri has soccer practice too, then."

"Mommy, please," Lela begged, but they would hear nothing more of it.

Tangled with Lela

I was in a tangled mess. First, with Josh at school and now with Lela. And if Josh and I didn't behave better the next day, Mr. Bugsby was going to tie us together again.

Lela pulled to the left while I pulled in the opposite direction.

"Where are you going?" I asked.

"Upstairs."

"I don't want to go upstairs."

"Zuri, we have to work together."

"You're not going to the bathroom, are you?"

46

"No."

"Don't lie, WOMAN. You can't poop with me attached to you."

"Ugh, why are you so annoying? I don't have to use the bathroom," said Lela.

Walking was harder with Lela than with Josh because she was taller. Our legs had step together to climb the stairs, with Lela holding the wall and me holding the banister.

At the top of the stairs, I tried to turn to go into Lela's room, but she pulled me toward the bathroom.

"I thought you didn't have to use it."

"I don't."

She removed a spray bottle from the cabinet under the sink with her free arm. "I'm making a detangler for my hair."

"Ooo... really?" I got excited. "Why didn't you say so in the first place? What do you need me to do?"

"You're going to have to hold the bottle still while I pour in the apple cider vinegar."

"Vinegar like we eat on cucumbers?"

"A different kind," Lela replied.

"Apple cider vinegar mixed with water detangles hair."

"It does?"

"That's what I just told you, sheesh."

"So can you use any kind of apple cider vinegar?" I asked.

"It has to have mother in it."

"Mother? Whose mother is in it? That's murder. Mommy!" I screeched.

"Oh my gosh. It's not a person." She held the bottle up. "Look. Do you see that brown stuff?"

"It looks like it's gone bad."

"No. That's called mother. It's like bacteria and protein and stuff. It's fine." Lela added two caps full of apple cider vinegar to the bottle, turned on the faucet, and filled the rest of the bottle with water. "Done."

"That's it? No vitamins or anything? What's next?"

Lela laughed. "You mean like the fish oil vitamins you added to garlic butter when you were trying to make hair butter? No, it doesn't need anything else. I'll spray it on my hair when I shower."

"And that detangles it?"

"Yep, and it will make my hair softer too."

I tapped my finger on my chin as I thought. I had a big idea and needed to discuss it with Pickle. But I didn't think she wanted to talk to me after the way I acted.

When it was time for bed, my mom found us in the family room. We were sitting on the floor watching a superhero movie in silence and sharing a bowl of popcorn.

"Okay, okay. You guys are free. That's the most peaceful evening I've had in a long time. You did good," she said as she untied us.

I grinned.

"She meant me," said Lela.

"Both of you."

I stuck my tongue out at Lela. My mom pushed it back in my mouth as she turned me in the opposite direction. "Bed. Now. Before you ruin it."

Friends Again

When I got off the school bus the next day, Pickle flew overhead. I grinned and then frowned. I couldn't be happy to see her anymore. We weren't friends. She was probably looking for Neli, not me.

I walked home and didn't look up at the drone again. When it landed on my lawn, I walked right past it and into the house.

An hour later, I looked outside, and the drone was still there, next to the palm tree.

Later that afternoon, I brought it inside. Then my cell phone rang.

"Hello, Zuri?" Gran said.

THUMP! THUMP!

That was the sound of my heart beating fast and loud. Gran only called on my phone when something was wrong. "Gran, what is it?"

"I need you to get over here fast."

"Fast?"

"Right now."

Gran hung up and I stared at my phone. "PICKLE!"

I ran to the garage door. "Mommy, Gran needs me. I'll be right back." I jumped on my scooter and kicked fast, all the way to Pickle's house. I sped past Noah and Kai, and then Omari.

"Zuri, what's wrong!" yelled Omari.

"Pickle," I screamed.

When I stopped in front of Pickle's house, I wasn't alone. Omari, Noah, Kai, and Hector, had followed me there.

"The front door is open," said Omari. "Did the ambulance come?"

"I don't know."

I ran up the ramp to the porch and Gran walked up to the screen door.

"There you are. That was fast. Come in."

The other kids waited as I walked inside. I was scared to go any further. I didn't want to see Pickle injured. But when I turned to the living room. Pickle rolled in on her wheelchair.

I looked up at Gran. "But... I thought—"

"You two need to talk. They'll be out in a minute," Gran told our friends waiting outside.

Pickle looked down at her lap.

We were quiet like we didn't know what to say. So I went first.

"Pickle, I'm sorry. But it's all your fault."

"No, it's not. Neli only lives across the street. Don't you have other friends on your end of the street, in the cul-de-sac?"

"Yes, but what has that got to do with anything? I can't help that I'm popular."

"I can have more than one friend just like you do."

I frowned at her.

Pickle continued. "But you are my very best friend in the entire world."

"Galaxy," I corrected.

"Yes, in the entire galaxy."

"Universe."

Pickle sighed and shook her head. "Okay, in the entire universe. Sheesh, can you stop it?"

"There is one thing you can do to make it up to me," I said.

"What's that?"

"Help me make my detangler."

"You have a new hair product invention?"

"Yessiree and you would've known about it had you not been lollygagging around with Neli." I learned that word from Gran. Lollygagging was a funny word.

"Yay, it's about time. When are we going to work on it?"

"I'll go home and get everything."

I ran to the door, and then ran back and hugged her. "Sorry, Pickle."

I hurried outside.

"Is she okay?" asked Kai.

"It was a false alarm, people!"

"See, I knew we shouldn't have come all the way down here," Noah whined. "Let's go."

Detangler

My mom grinned at me when I walked in the house. "Pickle's okay, I gather?"

"She sure is," I said as I ran by. "I'm just getting my backpack."

I grabbed the bottle of apple cider vinegar from the bathroom, put it in my backpack, and ran back to my scooter.

Pickle was waiting on her ramp when I arrived.

"Ready to make magic? Come on," I said.

She followed me inside. Looking just as excited as I felt. I set the bottle of apple cider vinegar on the kitchen counter.

"Eww... what's that brown cloudy stuff?" asked Pickle.

"It has the vinegar's mother in it."

"What?" Pickle asked as she giggled. "That doesn't sound right."

"Something like that. Anyway, all I have to do is mix it with water and spray it in your hair like so." I sprayed my empty spray bottle at her shooting air in her face.

She laughed. "And what does it do?"

"It makes your hair shiny and soft." I poured half the bottle of vinegar into the spray bottle and added two splashes of water from a water bottle. Then I shook it and held it up for Pickle to see.

She wrinkled her nose and coughed. "Smells kind of strong."

"That means we made a good one."

"I don't think we should use it on our hair. We keep getting in trouble about hair stuff."

The doorbell rang. I hid behind a chair. "That might be Lela looking for her vinegar."

"Who is it?" Pickle sang.

"Pickle, did Zuri come back over here?"

"Omari," we both said with a grin.

I ran to the screen door and let him in. "You're right on time, buddy—just who we were looking for."

"On time for what?"

"On time for a little experiment."

"Zuri, not again."

"No, no, no. It's already made, and I just need to spray a little on your hair."

"On *my* hair? No."

"What, are you chicken? BAWK, BAWK, BAWK!"

Pickle joined in with me. "BAWK, BAWK, BAWK!"

"I better not get in trouble."

"You won't."

Omari didn't have a lot of hair. But a short afro was just enough to test out our detangler.

"I don't know about this, Zuri. I'm not even a Curly Girl, and I don't want to be. And no, I will not go home and get my cat again."

"Just sit down and relax, Omari. We're going to fix you right up. Are you hungry? We can get you a—"

"Pickle," Pickle said, finishing my sentence.

Omari shook his head. "Nope. I never want to see a pickle again, after that blender covered us in your pickled pudding."

Pickle thought for a moment. "Beef Jerky?"

"Beef Jerky?" I asked.

"Yes. My dad likes it. He says it's a protein snack."

"Uncle Frank eats weird stuff. How about it, Omari?"

"It's a guy snack," Pickle said and winked at me. "For muscles."

Did I ever say that Pickle was the smartest person I knew?

"Okay," Omari said slowly. "I'll have a beef whatever it is."

He sat back in his chair, bit down on the brown stick of dried meat and pulled hard. A piece broke off, and he chomped on that thing for like five minutes.

"Well?"

"I like it," he said as he chewed.

"Good." I covered him with a tablecloth like at the beauty salon. I knew they didn't use tablecloths, but it was all I had.

"Just keep your eyes on the television Omari, and I will make Chuck beautiful."

"Who is Chuck?" he asked looking around.

"That's the name I'm giving your hair."

"My hair doesn't need a name, and I don't want to be beautiful. Hurry up."

"Okay, okay. We will make your hair soft." I winked at Pickle.

"Go ahead, Pickle!"

She held the spray bottle up and spritzed the detangler over the back of Omari's hair. "There."

"I think he needs more," I said as I shook the detangler up and sprayed a whole bunch of it all over Omari's head.

"Phew, that's strong," said Pickle.

She was right. It was much stronger than what Lela's smelled like. Her sprays didn't cause my eyes to sting.

Some of the detangler ran down Omari's forehead and into his face.

"My eyes are burning," he screamed and jumped up, dropping his jerky. "And my nose."

"Get him to the sink!" Pickle yelled.

"Hold on, Omari. You're okay." I turned on the faucet and used the sprayer nozzle to spray cold water over Omari's entire head and face. That guy coughed and gagged. He acted like I was drowning him.

"Zuri, what are you doing?" asked Gran as she hurried into the kitchen. We stood there with Omari dripping wet and rubbing his eyes.

"I tell ya, you kids are always getting into something," Gran said, as she dried Omari's face and head with a dishtowel.

His eyes were red.

"Zuri, you need to apologize. This is not how you treat your friends."

My head dropped. "I was only trying to— Sorry, Omari."

"It's okay. I should've known better."

I tugged at Gran's arm. "Are you going to tell your son?"

"You mean your father?" she asked.

I nodded.

Gran studied me for a moment, and I held my breath.

"No."

I hugged her as tight as I could.

Gran lifted my head and looked into my eyes. "You have to promise me, though. No more experimenting."

I gasped. "But I have to make stuff. It's the way I am."

"Not with children and not without an adult."

"But I didn't use anything electrical this time."

"Zuri…"

"Okay."

"Besides, I can't have you grounded on my birthday," Gran added.

"It's your birthday?"

I looked over at Pickle, and she nodded.

"It sure is," Gran said with a grin.

"But I didn't know. I didn't get you a gift or make a card."

I thought for a moment. "Then I really promise. No more experimenting. That's my gift to you."

Gran laughed. "I'll take it. That's the best gift I could ask for."

Behind me, Pickle hit my hand down, knocking away my crossed fingers.

All of our family came over for Gran's birthday dinner. Uncles and aunts, nieces, nephews, and cousins. Gran enjoyed her favorite meal of oxtails, rice, and steamed cabbage. My mom made her favorite desserts: sour cream pound cake and peach cobbler.

Omari and Neli came over, and Uncle Frank helped us make s'mores over the firepit in the backyard. My s'more was perfect. The marshmallow didn't get too burned and the chocolate square wasn't too melty.

We had so much fun. The party ended so late into the evening that my parents let me spend the night at Pickle's. There was a twin bed in her room just for me, and I always kept a change of clothes there.

In the morning, we ate cake for breakfast. "Just this one time," said Gran. That's because Pickle was on a special diet. I think it's called anti-inflamed. It helped her to not have pain. I think her body can make flames on the inside or something. I hoped the cake wouldn't hurt her.

BAM, BAM, BAM!

The sound came from down the hall. I followed it. "Uncle Frank, what are you doing? What's all of that noise?"

"This here is an antique wardrobe that I got your Gran for her birthday. It needed a few repairs, and then I will polish it up." He motioned for me to come closer. "Look at the lions engraved in the doors."

I ran my fingers over the carvings. "It's beautiful. Do you need any help?"

"Thank you for asking, but I think I've got it."

"But I can hand you stuff."

"Do you know tools?"

"I sure do. I help Daddy sometimes."

"Then hand me the Phillips-head screwdriver."

I looked in the toolbox. "Got it, Uncle Frank. Here you go."

"Zuri, that's a wrench."

"Oops. I'm better with hair stuff."

Gran's Birthday Gift

Pickle and I stood in front of Gran's polished closet and looked at each other, a smile crept across our faces.

"Are you thinking what I'm thinking?" Pickle asked.

"This looks like…"

"I know…"

I turned to her. "Do you think?"

"I don't know."

"Should we check?" I asked while holding the knob of the wardrobe. "No. Wait. Let's call Omari and everyone over.

Ten minutes later, Noah, Kai, Omari, Neli, and Hector joined us in front of Gran's closet.

"Do you really think it will take us to a magical land like in the book or the movie?" asked Hector

"That's childish," said Kai.

"We *are* children," Pickle replied.

"What if it can, though?" I asked.

"No, it can't," said Noah.

"What are you kids doing in here?" Gran asked as she walked into the room.

"Looking at your wardrobe. Have you put anything in there yet?" I asked.

"Coats and blankets, why?"

"Have you noticed anything weird about it?"

"Define weird."

"Did you see something inside. Something that's not supposed to be in there?"

"You think it's haunted, Zuri?" Gran asked. "Is that the problem? Are you children afraid of it?"

"No, no, no, Gran. Not ghosts. Did you see animals in there or a fairytale land?"

Gran couldn't stop laughing. "That's why all of you are in my room?" She opened the closet and we jumped back. One by one we stepped forward and pulled her coats out of the way.

"See." Gran moved the blankets around. "It's just the back of the wardrobe."

"That's what adults always see," I whispered.

Zuri's Dream

That night I dreamed of Gran's closet. I climbed inside and Pickle followed me. She could walk as good as I in my dream. The back wall changed right before our eyes and we walked right through it.

"The copper people of Fantastica have been captured and we need to save them. There is going to be a grand celebration afterward. They need you, Zuri," an ant man said.

There were trees of every color, and instead of blue, the sky was in bright rainbow colors.

The copper people that hadn't been captured bowed as we approached. They looked like pennies.

"Zuri the Great, thank you for returning to our kingdom. The frog king has teamed up with the Palmetto armies and captured the people of the north country."

"Don't worry. We will bring them back, Your Highness," said Pickle.

"Be careful of the Barbie giants who guard the boundaries."

"Don't worry King Cent. We've got this."

"They could be anywhere, Pickle. Be careful."

I squatted next to the green and purple oyster plants that surrounded a palm tree and spread apart the leaves.

"Don't go in there!" yelled Pickle. "It's a trap!"

Five raccoons wearing armor and carrying swords jumped out at me.

I ran across the open field screaming and fighting off those bad guys.

Pickle karate chopped at them.

"Pickle do you hear that chittering sound?"

"Yes. What is that?"

"They're calling for backup."

Pickle and I backed toward the edge of the forest. The raccoons had us cornered.

"Pickle, look!" Thousands of copper people rolled into action to help us.

"Charge!" I yelled, and we moved on to rescue the people of the north country and pounced on the Palmetto army.

The inhabitants of Fantastica gave us crowns and had a whole parade in our honor.

I awoke happy and with a great idea. I couldn't wait to go to Pickle's house to check out Gran's wardrobe. But my mom made huevos rancheros for breakfast, and it was important that I get my nourishment first.

"What are you in such a hurry about?" asked Lela.

I stuffed a large fork of eggs and corn tortilla in my mouth and spoke as I chewed. "You don't want to know about it. You're too old."

"Tell me."

"Have you seen Gran's new wardrobe?"

"I heard about it."

"But have you *seen* it?" I asked.

"Why? What's so special about it?"

I shook my head, drank the rest of my juice, and placed my dishes in the sink. "I'm going to Gran's, Mommy!"

"Wait, I'm going with you," Lela yelled behind me.

While she ran up the stairs to get her shoes, I called Pickle. "We're on the way."

"Roger that," she responded.

What's in There

"It's pretty," Lela said as we stood in front of the wardrobe. "I don't see why you wanted to come over here and stare at it, though. "Am I missing something, Zuri?"

"Doesn't it look familiar to you?"

Lela stepped closer. She had to see it. It was her favorite movie.

She chuckled. "Now I get it. It does resemble Professor Digory's magical wardrobe, but that's not real. You're acting like such a child. You thought you could go inside, and the wardrobe would act as a portal to Narnia? You need to grow up."

I stared at the closet and stepped back.

"What's wrong with you?" Lela asked.

I kept my eyes on the closet

Something moved around inside. It pushed at the door.

"What was that? That stuff isn't real!" Lela shrieked.

"Pickle!" I screamed.

She rolled in on her wheelchair. "What's going on?" she said and gasped hearing the movement. "What's in there?"

I looked at her with my eyeballs bulging. "I don't know. Someone's coming through from another land, I think."

"Th-that's not possible," Lela stuttered.

I pushed her toward the wardrobe. "Then open it."

"No, I can't. You're the one who's supposed to be Zuri the Great. You open it."

"I-I don't feel so great right now," I said as I backed away.

Lela pulled me. "You stay right there."

"Why? Are you scared?"

She shook her head and jumped hearing a pound on the door.

Lela tiptoed to the wardrobe, and I followed close behind. She placed her hand on the knob and pulled. The door slowly opened, and we waited.

Neli popped out with a growl.

Lela screamed and jumped across the room.

Gran had been in the hall waiting and walked in laughing.

Pickle laughed so hard, there were tears in her eyes.

Neli fell over on the floor laughing.

"You almost gave me a heart attack, Woman!" I yelled, with a big smile on my face.

"That was so wrong," Lela said, catching her breath.

I high-fived Pickle. "Payback!"

Lela grinned. "Okay, you got me. That was a good one."

A Curly Girl

Surprise

That evening, Lela and my mom stood near the stove talking. "Why are you guys whispering?" I asked.

They wouldn't tell me. That woman was going to try to get me back for tricking her, I was sure.

Lela spoke louder to my mom. "Eshay otewray atthay."

"I can understand Pig Latin, you know."

Lela turned to me with her hand on her hip. "Yeah? Then what did I say?"

"Eat oats on a tray."

...

I tried not to get into anymore arguments with Lela, so I wouldn't have to get tangled up with her again.

At school, it was much harder. Beetle-faced Josh kept bothering me, but I didn't snap. That kid didn't mind being tangled up with me.

"Just ignore him," said Omari.

Zoey ran up to us, "You better leave her alone or I'm telling."

"Go and tell," said Josh as he jumped around us.

"Class," said Mr. Bugsby.

Zoey and Omari went back to their desks.

Mr. Bugsby had a really happy look. "Class, someone has a birthday today."

The students clapped as they looked around at each other, trying to figure out whose birthday it was.

I slammed my fists on my desk.

"If you read quietly, we'll get set up here in just a bit," Mr. Bugsby continued.

I turned to Omari. "Is it your birthday?"

He shook his head, and so did all the kids in our row.

I turned to Josh. "I'll be nicer to you today since it's your birthday."

That kid had a huge grin. It wasn't a happy grin. It was a sneaky grin.

I looked up at Mr. Bugsby, and he pointed at my book. As soon as I started reading, I heard someone enter the classroom.

"Ooo," some of the kids said.

I refused to look up at him or her. I was trying to be good, but I didn't want another party at school until I had one. I held the book up over my face, so I couldn't see Josh's mom.

"Thank you," said Josh, all happy-like. I knew they were handing out cupcakes or slices of cake. Of course he would be good in front of his mother.

I stared at my book, but I wasn't reading.

"Don't you want a cupcake?"

I recognized that voice and looked up with my mouth hanging open. "Mommy?"

"Yes?"

I was so happy I started crying, and I don't even know why.

"Hey," she said as she hugged me.

"Thank you for my birthday."

"I didn't know how you felt about having a party at school until Lela told me."

"Lela did something nice for me?"

"She saw your list," my mom said. "You have to learn to tell people how you feel about things. Even about your birthday. The date won't change. But every once in a while, we can make an exception. So this isn't really a birthday party, but a special gift for being nicer to Josh and Lela."

"Yeah, because I don't want to be tangled up with that guy anymore."

"I've learned my lesson, too," said Josh, with a mouth filled with the purple frosting of his cupcake.

"I think that deserves another cupcake—for everybody," said my mom.

"YAY!" the class exclaimed.

"He's not telling the truth," I whispered.

Then Josh burped real loud making all the boys laugh. But I didn't let him shake my nerves.

My mom stayed for the rest of the afternoon and got to meet the new Curly Girl, Zoey.

She sat next to me and I pinched her.

"Ouch!" my mom exclaimed. "What did you do that for?"

I raised my hand. "Oh Mr. Bugsby! I think I need to be tangled up with my mom."

**THANK YOU FOR READING
TANGLED**

**Please consider leaving a review.
One or two sentences is great.
It helps other readers find out about the
Curly Girl Adventures series.
Thank you so much!**

Five more
things you
didn't know
about
L B. Anne

1. I don't like scary movies.
2. Christmas is my favorite
   holiday.
3. The beach is my happy place.
4. My favorite place to visit is
   Scotland.
5. Smoothie bowls are my
   favorite snack.

ABOUT THE AUTHOR

L B. Anne is best known for her Lolo and Winkle book series in which she tells humorous stories of middle-school siblings, Lolo and Winkle, based on her youth, growing up in Queens, New York. She lives on the Gulf Coast of Florida with her husband and is a full-time author and speaker. When she's not inventing new obstacles for her diverse characters to overcome, you can find her reading, playing bass guitar, running on the beach, or downing a mocha iced coffee at a local cafe while dreaming of being your favorite author.

Stay in touch at www.lbanne.com

Facebook: facebook.com/authorlbanne

Instagram: Instagram.com/authorlbanne

Twitter: twitter.com/authorlbanne

Made in the USA
Middletown, DE
13 November 2024

64537487R00057